THE PRINCESS AND THE PEA

THE PRINCESS AND THE PEA

Retold and illustrated by

Sucie Stevenson

A Picture Yearling Book

Published by Dell Publishing
a division of
Bantam Doubleday Dell Publishing Group, Inc.
1540 Broadway
New York, New York 10036

The trademark Yearling® is registered in the U.S. Patent and
Trademark Office.
The trademark Dell® is registered in the U.S. Patent and
Trademark Office.
ISBN: 0-440-40964-0

Reprinted by arrangement with Doubleday Books for
Young Readers

Printed in the United States of America

August 1994

3 5 7 9 10 8 6 4

DAN

For Brad Brooks,
of Kansas

Once upon a time there was a prince who wanted a princess.

But he wanted to make sure that she was a *real* princess.

He traveled all over the world to find one.

There were plenty of princesses, but the prince could not be sure they were *real* ones.

There was always something about them that was not quite right.

Finally he returned home with no princess at all. He was very sad because he began to worry that he would never find a real princess.

One evening there was a terrible storm. There was thunder and lightning, and the rain poured down in sheets. It was just dreadful.

Suddenly the royal family heard a banging at the castle gates. The old king himself went to see who it could be.

Imagine how surprised he was to see a princess standing there.
But goodness gracious! What a sight she was, drenched from the
rain.

Water dripped from her hair and her clothes. It ran down into the toes of her shoes and out again at the heels.
Yet she said that she was a real princess.

"Well, we'll just see about that," thought the old queen.

She said nothing, but went into a guest room and took all the bedding off the bed. She placed a pea at the bottom.

Then she had twenty mattresses stacked on top of the pea and
twenty eiderdown quilts piled on top of that.

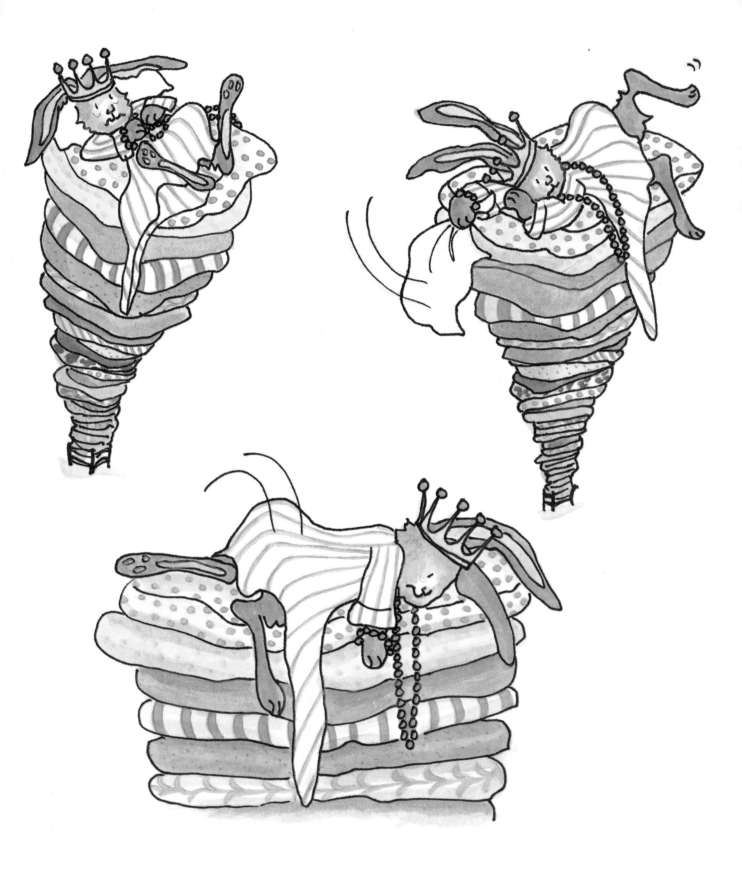

The princess had to lie there all night.

In the morning the old queen asked the princess how she had slept.
"I did not sleep one bit the whole night," said the princess.
"Heaven only knows what was in the bed, but it was so hard that I am black-and-blue all over. I need a nap."

The royal family was thrilled. Now they knew that she was a real princess because she had felt the pea right through the twenty mattresses and the twenty eiderdown quilts.

Nobody but a real princess could have done that.

So the prince took her for his wife.

And the pea was put in a crystal case in the royal museum,

where it can still be seen—if no one has stolen it.

Now that is a real story!

The End.